Usborne First Experiences

Moving house

Anne Civardi

Edited by Michelle Bates

Illustrated by Stephen Cartwright

Cover design by Jan McCafferty

There is a little yellow duck hiding on every double page. Can you find it?

This is the Spark family.

Sam is seven and Sophie is five. They are moving into a new house very soon.

This is the Sparks' old house.

They have sold it to Mr. and Mrs. Potts. The Potts have come today to measure the rooms.

The Sparks go to see their new house.

The house is being painted before the Sparks move in. Mr. Spark makes friends with the people who live next door.

Two men from Cosy Carpets arrive to put new carpets down in some of the rooms.

The Sparks pack up their old house.

It takes many days for Mr. and Mrs. Spark to sort out all of their things. Packing is hard work.

Sam makes sure that all of his things are packed too. But Sophie would rather play.

The Sparks move.

Frank

Bill

Early in the morning, a big removal truck arrives to take the Sparks' furniture to their new home.

Bill, the driver, and Frank and Bess, his helpers, load everything into the big truck. Then they drive it to the new house.

Everyone helps unload the truck.

Bill shows Sam and Sophie the inside of the truck. Then they all start to take the things into the new house.

They take things inside.

Bill, Frank and Bess carry the heavy furniture into the house. Mrs. Spark shows them where to put everything.

This is Sophie's new bedroom.

Dad helps Sophie to get it ready. He puts up the curtains. Sophie is very excited about having a new room.

Sam has his own room too.

Sam likes the new house. Now he does not have to share a room with Sophie. Mrs. Spark helps him unpack.

The Sparks meet the people from next door.

In the afternoon the Sparks go for a walk down their street. There are lots of people to meet.

Mrs. Tobbit

Sophie and Sam will have some new friends to play with. Mrs. Tobbit from next door gives Mr. Spark a big cake to welcome them.

The Sparks go to bed.

Mr. and Mrs. Spark, Sophie and Sam are very tired after the move.

They fall fast asleep in their new home.

First published in 1992. This revised edition published in 2000 by Usborne Publishing Ltd, Usborne House, 83-85 Saffron Hill, London EC1N 8RT, England
Copyright © 2000, 1992 Usborne Publishing Ltd.
First published in America in 2001
The name Usborne and the device ⊕ are Trade Marks of Usborne Publishing Ltd.